BIG BUG SURPRISE

JULIA GRAN

Scholastic Press ✸ New York

Prunella was busy as a bee getting ready for school.

She had an important decision to make.

Which of her favorite bugs should

she bring for show-and-tell?

At breakfast, Prunella told her parents,
"Did you know that
spiders are not insects?
Insects always have six legs,
but spiders have eight legs."

"Not now, Prunella," said her parents.

On the bus,
Prunella informed the bus driver,
"Dragonflies are the fastest insects.
They can fly up to sixty miles per hour.
That's faster than our school bus!"

"Not now, Prunella," said the bus driver.

At school, Prunella ran to her teacher.

"Ms. Mantis," she said, "do you want to see my show-and-tell?"

"Not now, Prunella," said Ms. Mantis.

"Class, take your seats."

All morning,
Prunella wondered,
"Will it ever be time
for show-and-tell?"

Finally, it was time!
But since Prunella
sat in the last seat,
in the last row,
she had to **wait**
and
wait
and
wait.
Until . . .

"Prunella," called Ms. Mantis, "it's your turn."

Prunella carried her show-and-tell to the front of the class.

Just then, a bug flew in the window.

"Fascinating," said Prunella. "That's a queen bee.

They never fly alone."

"Not now, Prunella," said Ms. Mantis.

All of a sudden, the classroom filled with bees, bees, and more bees!

"They must be looking for a new hive," said Prunella.

"NOT NOW, PRUNELLA!" said Ms. Mantis.

Everyone ran
except Prunella.
She said,
"I know what to do."

Prunella grabbed her jelly sandwich
and the sheet she'd used to
cover her show-and-tell.

Then, through the classroom door,
down the hallway,
across the playground,
Prunella led the bees out of the school.

"**PRUNELLA!**" called Ms. Mantis.
"What are you doing? Be careful!"

"Don't worry, Ms. Mantis," said Prunella,
"the bees can't see me while I am covered in white.
Bees don't sting what they don't see.

"This looks like a good spot.
Welcome to your new hive."

"WOW!"
"COOL!"
"AMAZING!"
cheered the class.

"You see, bees love sweets," said Prunella, "so I attracted the queen with my jelly sandwich. And since bees follow their queen anywhere, I brought her to the tree."

"That's very interesting, Prunella," said Ms. Mantis.

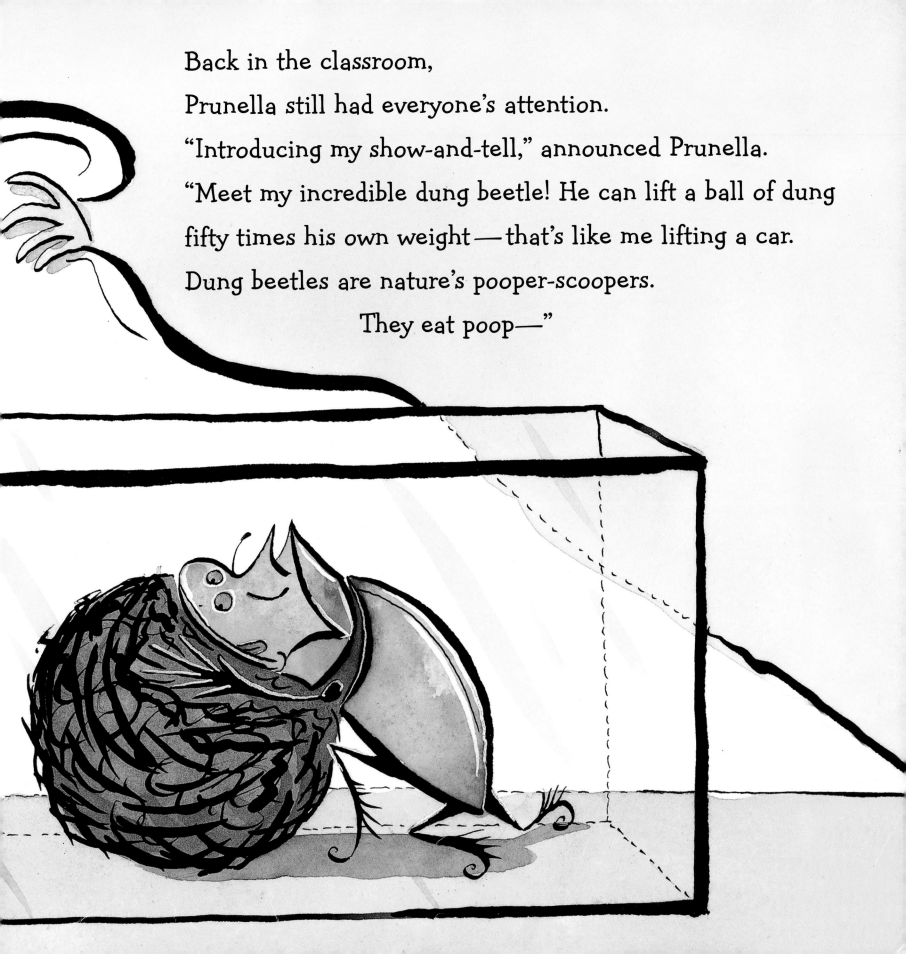

Back in the classroom,

Prunella still had everyone's attention.

"Introducing my show-and-tell," announced Prunella.

"Meet my incredible dung beetle! He can lift a ball of dung

fifty times his own weight—that's like me lifting a car.

Dung beetles are nature's pooper-scoopers.

They eat poop—"

"GACK!"

"NASTY!"

"TELL US MORE,
PRUNELLA,"
said the class.

And, of course, she did.

BIG BUG FACTS

INSECTS are the largest animal group on earth. They have six legs, two antennae, and most have wings. They eat more plants than all the other animals on earth. Without insects, the earth would be covered with dead plants and animals! Dragonflies, honeybees, and dung beetles are insects:

DRAGONFLIES eat gnats, flies, and mosquitoes. Their eyes are positioned on the sides of their heads so they can see 360 degrees. Imagine that while you look forward you can see behind you, too. That's how a dragonfly sees.

HONEYBEES make honey and beeswax. They pollinate plants that produce fruits and vegetables. As many as 60,000 bees live in a group called a colony. A colony has a queen, workers (females), and drones (males). Bees sting if they feel threatened. If a bee approaches, always remain calm. That can prevent your being stung. Never approach a hive or handle bees unless you are with an adult who has experience keeping bees.

DUNG BEETLES live on animal excrement, or dung (poop!). They clean up the environment by collecting the dung, rolling it into balls, and burying the dung balls. They can smell fresh dung up to ten miles away. Farting cows are like a dinner bell for the dung beetle.

SPIDERS have eight legs, no wings, and as many as eight eyes. They have fangs and spin silk webs as a tool for hunting. Spiders are not insects—they're arachnids.

TO MY FATHER, MY MOTHER, AND MY SISTER

Copyright © 2007 by Julia Gran · All rights reserved. Published by Scholastic Press, an imprint of Scholastic Inc., *Publishers since 1920.* · SCHOLASTIC, SCHOLASTIC PRESS, and associated logos are trademarks and/or registered trademarks of Scholastic Inc. · No part of this publication may be reproduced, stored in a retrieval system, or transmitted in any form or by any means, electronic, mechanical, photocopying, recording, or otherwise, without written permission of the publisher. For information regarding permission, write to Scholastic Inc., Attention: Permissions Department, 557 Broadway, New York, NY 10012. · Library of Congress Cataloging-in-Publication Data: Gran, Julia. Big bug surprise / by Julia Gran. — 1st ed. p. cm. Summary: Prunella knows so much about insects that people get bored listening to her talk, but when her classroom fills up with bees during show-and-tell, Prunella saves the day. Includes facts about insects. ISBN-13: 978-0-439-67609-0 ISBN-10: 0-439-67609-6 (hardcover) [1. Insects—Fiction. 2. Bees—Fiction. 3. Show-and-tell presentations—Fiction. 4. Schools—Fiction.] I. Title. PZ7. G77565Pru 2007 [E]—dc22 2006004605 · 10 9 8 7 6 5 4 3 2 1 · 07 08 09 10 11 12 · Printed in Singapore · 46 · First edition, February 2007 · Book design by Alison Klapthor

JP   Gran, Julia.

            Big bug surprise.